YOU ARE 7 AND
AMAZING

Inspiring Stories For 7 Year Old Boys

15 Motivating Tales of Bravery,
Self Confidence, Friendships
and Adventure

Mary Allan

CONTENTS

INTRODUCTION

Dear Amazing 7-year-old,

Did you know that 7-year-olds are like adventure experts, discovering new things and having the most fun while doing them?

It's so great to be seven because every day, you're trying new challenges and finding out how awesome you are.

This book is full of fifteen kids just like you—each with their own exciting story to share. You'll join them in building forts, chasing stars, and taking on daring secret missions. You'll laugh at their silly moments, cheer for their big wins, and feel inspired by how they face their challenges. From wobbly towers to thrilling adventures, every story is packed with fun, surprises, and a lesson to take with you.

Discover stories where teamwork turns challenges into victories, kindness sparks unexpected friendships, and a little patience leads to incredible surprises. You'll find that being seven is all about creating amazing memories.

So, what are you waiting for? Let's begin! These stories will make your year of being seven even more incredible!

BEST FORT EVER

"No, no, it has to be BIGGER!" Ezra insisted, waving his arms as he imagined the towering walls of the fort in his backyard. It was a perfect day for building. His friends, Daniel, Leo, and Sophie, had brought everything they could find—cardboard boxes, old blankets, and even a few long sticks.

"We need a secret tunnel on this side," Daniel said, tugging a cardboard box toward the middle.

"But it should be low, so no one can see us from far away," Leo added, crouching as he measured the ground with his hands.

Sophie held up a fluffy blanket. "What about a cozy corner inside, like a hideout?"

Ezra's excitement began to fade. Each of his friends had their own ideas, and none of them included his plan for a lookout tower. *But what's the point of a fort without a tall tower?* he mumbled to himself.

Still, they started building, each working on their own part. Daniel went to one side, trying to secure his tunnel. Leo stacked short sticks into a low wall around the fort, while Sophie spread out her blanket. Ezra began stacking boxes for his tower.

After a few minutes, it was clear that things weren't working. Daniel's tunnel kept caving in, and Leo's walls wobbled. Ezra's stack of boxes was leaning dangerously to one side, and just as he added another on top, it all came tumbling down with a CRASH!

Ezra's clenched his fists. *This was supposed to be amazing!* he thought. Instead, it looked like a pile of random stuff. His friends all looked frustrated, too.

"Maybe… maybe we should stop," Sophie said, in a soft voice.

Ezra took a deep breath, trying to shake off his irritation. He looked at his friends' disappointed faces and realized they probably felt the same way he did. *I don't want to give up. We've come this far,* he thought.

"Wait! What if we try building it together?" Ezra said. "We can include everyone's ideas. We could make a short tower that's still easy to climb, add the tunnel on one side, and put Sophie's cozy blanket inside!"

The group exchanged glances, considering the new plan. Then, one by one, they nodded. Working together, they had found a way to combine everyone's ideas. Ezra helped secure Daniel's tunnel with rocks and sticks, and Leo used Ezra's boxes to make the walls steadier. Sophie created a little nook with her blanket, adding pillows they found in the house. What a team!

Once the fort was finished, the friends huddled inside, catching their breath. The walls felt sturdy, the cozy corner was perfect, and Daniel's tunnel was just wide enough for them to crawl through. They looked around when suddenly, an idea popped into Ezra's head.

"What if... this isn't just a fort?" Ezra said, lowering his voice to a whisper, his eyes shining brightly. "What if it's a pirate ship, and we're sailing through dangerous seas!"

Daniel jumped up, pretending to grab a telescope. "Aye, Aye, Captain! I see land ahead, but... oh no! There's a sea monster blocking our way!"

The others squealed, all playing along as the sea monster 'roared' and lashed its 'tentacles' at the ship—really just some long sticks poking through the side of the fort.

Leo scrambled to the 'ship's' edge, holding a stick like a sword. "I'll fight it off!" he shouted, swinging his stick at the imaginary monster. Sophie, laughing, grabbed a pillow from her cozy corner and used it as a 'shield,' braving the storm with her friends.

"Hold on tight, everyone!" Ezra shouted, gripping an imaginary wheel and steering the fort-turned-ship through wild, invisible waves. They swayed side to side, ducking and dodging as they defeated the sea monster together.

Finally, with one last cheer, they 'sailed' safely past the monster and spotted land. They all let out a big sigh of relief, grinning from ear to ear.

"Best. Fort. Ever!" Daniel declared, flopping back onto the blanket, out of breath but beaming.

As they settled back down, Ezra realized something new and pretty important—when they worked together, their fort really could be anything they imagined. And with friends by his side, there was no adventure too big to take on.

Now that you are seven, remember that great things happen when we work together and let our imaginations run wild!

BIG SOCCER COMEBACK

"Remember, just play your best!" Axel's mom called from the sidelines as he jogged onto the field. Her words were hard to hear over all the noise around him. He nodded, but he couldn't stop the heavy feeling in his chest from last week's tough loss. Axel glanced at his best friend Gavin, who looked just as nervous.

"Think we'll do better next time?" Gavin asked, adjusting his shin guards.

"I hope so," Axel replied, trying to sound more confident than he felt. Just then, Coach Miles called the team over.

"Alright, team," Coach Miles began, holding up a small box. "Today, we're trying something new. Inside this box are some 'challenges'—little skills you'll work on for the week. Some are fun, and some might be tricky, but they're all meant to help you become better players."

The kids exchanged curious looks as Coach Miles passed around the box, each taking a slip of paper. When it was Axel's turn, he opened his paper and saw two words staring back at him: 'Spin Move.'

Axel's heart sank. He had seen players do the spin move in videos, but it looked so difficult and...well, impossible. "Gavin, look," he said, showing his friend the paper.

Gavin grinned, holding up his own paper that read, 'Ball Control.'

"You got this, Axel! It'll be cool once you get it down."

At first, Axel's attempts at the spin move felt like a disaster. He tried to twist with the ball at his feet, but he'd lose his balance or accidentally kick the ball too far. After a few tries, he sat down on the grass, feeling super annoyed at himself.

"Hey, don't give up yet," Gavin said, bouncing his own ball. "Coach said we'd get better with practice, right?"

With a sigh, Axel stood up and tried again. As the days passed, he practiced in his backyard most evenings. His dog, Chex, watched him from the side, tail wagging, almost as if cheering him on. Little by little, the spin move started to feel...not easy, but at least possible.

The next practice came around, and Axel felt some anxious feelings, but still excited. When Coach Miles called him to show his spin move, he took a deep breath, focused on the ball, and spun, just like he'd practiced. The move wasn't perfect, but he did it without tripping!

"Go, Axel!" his teammates cheered. Axel felt a lot better! But then, Coach Miles suggested trying it in a real game situation.

"Imagine you're in a game, with the other team right on you. Go!" Coach encouraged.

Axel's heart raced as he spun with the ball, but this time, he stumbled. The other players rushed in, taking the ball with ease. *AGHH!* He said to himself. *Maybe I'm just not meant for soccer.* After practice, he preferred to sit on the field by himself for a bit, running the events over in his mind.

At home that night, he told his mom about what happened. "It's so hard, Mom. I practiced and still messed up," he said, his voice shaky.

His mom sat on the bed next to him, putting her arm around him. "But think of how much you've already improved. You're learning, Axel. You've forgotten that it's about trying your best. Your best is always good enough."

Her words comforted him a little, but he still had that worrying feeling.

The day of the next game arrived, and Axel's stomach was filled with butterflies. As he stood on the field, he glanced down at his cleats and felt a tiny rush of courage. He repeated his mom's words silently, "Your best is good enough."

As the game began, Axel focused on his position, blocking a few passes and even managing to steal the ball once. But soon, the other team started scoring, and the gap grew wider. He could feel the tension rising.

Then, with just a few minutes left, a miracle happened—the ball bounced right in front of him. Axel froze. Doubts filled his mind. But then thoughts of all those nights he'd spent practicing swept the doubts away.

Here goes nothing…, he said to himself and went for the spin move. His body turned with the ball, his feet moved just like he'd practiced, and he felt the thrill as he slipped past two defenders!

He heard Gavin's voice, "Axel, pass it here!" Without thinking, he kicked the ball over to Gavin, who sprinted forward and took the shot. The ball soared into the net, and the entire team erupted in cheers. They hadn't won the game, but the goal sure felt like victory!

After the game, Coach Miles reached up for a high-five. "You didn't give up, Axel. That's what counts."

Gavin high-fived him too. "You rocked that spin move! Told you it'd pay off!"

As he looked over to the bleachers, Axel spotted his mom, clapping proudly. For the first time, he understood what his mom meant by doing his best. Winning or losing didn't matter as much as how he played.

Now that you are seven, remember doing your best means never giving up. Sometimes, it's the journey that makes you a true winner.

NIGHT AT THE OBSERVATORY

"Come on, Mom, we have to hurry!" Colin said as he tugged his mom's hand, practically pulling her into the observatory. The excitement buzzed inside him like a rocket ready to launch. He'd never been to an observatory before, and he was certain that tonight would be spectacular.

Inside, everything felt huge, and the hushed voices and dark shadows only made it more mysterious. People gazed up at stars through enormous telescopes, their faces glowing with wonder. Colin could barely wait for a second more.

"Are you ready to see the stars up close?" asked the guide, a friendly man with a big smile who led them to one of the largest telescopes in the room. Colin peered through, holding his breath, and there it was—a sky full of stars, glittering like they were waiting just for him.

"Look at that bright blue one!" Colin whispered, pointing. It was so clear that it felt like he could reach out and touch it.

"That's Vega," the guide explained. "Vega doesn't always appear in the same spot, but tonight, you're in luck. It's a rare sight."

Colin's eyes were glued to Vega, the tiny spark of blue. "Wow... I want to see Vega every night," he said quietly, feeling like he'd just discovered a secret. That night, on the drive home, his mind was spinning with ideas. He turned to his mom. "Do you think... maybe... I could find Vega from our backyard?"

The very next evening, Colin transformed his backyard into his own 'observatory.' He spread a blanket, gathered some snacks, and grabbed his mom's binoculars. He even had a little notebook to write down anything he found. His mom peeked out the window with a smile as he settled in, determined to find Vega.

I'm going to find you, Vega, he said to himself, lifting the binoculars to his eyes. The sky stretched out above him, vast and filled with stars he could barely see without the giant telescope.

He searched and searched, his binoculars scanning left, then right, but no Vega. Just some pretty twinkling dots scattered across the sky. He squinted harder, his fingers tightening around the binoculars. "Where are you, Vega?" he murmured.

Minutes turned into nearly an hour, and still, there was no sign of his special blue star. His arm grew tired from holding up the binoculars, and his eyelids began to droop. Just then, he noticed a few clouds creeping across the sky, blocking out some of the stars. "No, no, no... Not now!" he muttered, frustration fizzing up. Maybe this wasn't going to work after all.

For a moment, he thought about packing up and heading inside. He couldn't see Vega, his fingers were cold, and his excitement was starting to fade. But then he remembered what the guide had said: Vega didn't always appear in the same spot, and sometimes it took patience to see something amazing.

With a determined huff, Colin wrapped himself in his blanket and stayed put. "I'm not giving up on you, Vega," he said confidently to the sky.

After what felt like ages, the clouds began to drift away, leaving the sky clear again. Colin took a deep breath, lifting his binoculars one more time. His heart raced with hope. What if Vega finally appeared?

Just then, a faint shimmer of blue caught his eye. At first, he thought he was imagining it, but there it was—a tiny, twinkling blue light against the dark sky!

"Vega!" he gasped. It was even brighter and more magical than he'd remembered from the observatory. The whole world seemed to go quiet as he stared, feeling like the little blue star was shining just for him. The wait had been worth every single second.

Colin lay back on his blanket, a huge grin on his face, watching Vega twinkle. All the frustration he'd felt before faded away and was replaced by feeling very happy and very proud of himself. He'd done it. He'd found Vega.

When he finally headed inside, his mom greeted him with a proud smile. "Did you find it?"

"I did!" he said, his voice full of wonder. "I really did…"

She hugged him close. "Your patience really paid off, hey!"

Now that you are seven, you know that patience
can make big dreams come true, and the
best discoveries are worth waiting for.

HELPING IN GRANDPA'S WORKSHOP

Wyatt peeked excitedly around the corner of Grandpa's workshop. "Are you ready for our big project, Wyatt?" Grandpa asked, his face lighting up as he pointed to a pile of wood pieces stacked on the table. Wyatt's eyes popped wide. He couldn't believe it—they were going to build a birdhouse from scratch!

"I'm ready, Grandpa!" he said, but inside, he felt a little unsure. The workshop was packed with tools he'd only seen before in Grandpa's hands, and the idea of using them made him feel a bit nervous.

What if I make a mistake, drop it, or hurt myself? thought Wyatt.

Grandpa picked up a small piece of wood and handed Wyatt a piece of sandpaper. "First, we have to make everything smooth," he said, showing Wyatt how to sand. Wyatt nodded, grabbing his own piece and starting to rub it across the wood, feeling the roughness fade under his fingers. But just as he was getting the hang of it, the sandpaper slipped, and he almost dropped the wood.

"Oh no!" he muttered, frustration bubbling up. He wanted to be great at this, but it was harder than he'd thought. Grandpa smiled, patting his shoulder. "You're doing fine, Wyatt. I didn't get it perfect on my first try, either."

Wyatt gave a small grin, feeling a bit better. He picked up the sandpaper and kept going, slower this time, and was relieved when Grandpa nodded in approval. "Nice work! Now, let's move on to the hammering."

This is cool... thought Wyatt as Grandpa handed him a small nail and showed him how to hold it steady with one hand while he used the hammer in the other. But no sooner had he started than—bam!—the nail slipped sideways.

"Oops!" Wyatt mumbled, feeling a little embarrassed that he didn't get it right the first time. He tried again, only to have it slip a second time. He gritted his teeth. *Why is this so difficult?*

"Here, let me show you a little trick," Grandpa said, gently guiding Wyatt's hand. They hammered together, and the nail finally went in straight. Wyatt let out a sigh of relief and glanced at Grandpa with a thankful grin.

"Thanks, Grandpa. I thought I'd never get it right!"

Grandpa chuckled, "That's the thing about projects, Wyatt. Sometimes, you have to slow down and try a few times. I didn't get it right the first time either!"

They worked on the birdhouse for the next hour, sanding, nailing, and fitting pieces together. Just as they were about to attach the roof, Wyatt eagerly grabbed the first nail he saw, wanting to help get it finished. But as soon as he hammered it in, a sharp crack echoed in the workshop—the wood had split.

Wyatt's heart sank. "Oh no… Grandpa, I think I broke it!" He glanced up, feeling so sorry.

"It's okay, Wyatt," said Grandpa with a knowing smile. "Accidents happen. I've done that too! Now, let's see if we can fix it together."

Wyatt watched, amazed, as Grandpa showed him how to carefully remove the broken piece and replace it with a new one. His frustration faded away, though, as he realized that even little mistakes didn't ruin the project. Grandpa was teaching him to be patient, even when things went wrong.

After a few more steps, they were finished. Wyatt held up the birdhouse. "We did it, Grandpa! It looks amazing!" He couldn't believe they had started with just a pile of wood, and now they had this perfect little house for birds!

Grandpa grinned, slapping him playfully on the back. "You did well, Wyatt. Every little mistake was just part of the process."

Together, they carried the birdhouse outside to the big tree in Grandpa's yard. Grandpa lifted it high and hung it on a low branch, where it swayed gently in the breeze. They both stepped back to admire their work and as they did, a small bird fluttered over to investigate, its tiny eyes glancing curiously into the little wooden home.

Wyatt felt a mix of happiness and pride that made him want to smile forever. He glanced up at Grandpa, who was smiling as if he knew exactly what Wyatt was feeling.

"Thanks, Grandpa," he said. "For teaching me."

Grandpa nodded. "Anytime, Wyatt. Patience and teamwork can build wonderful things."

As they walked back to the house, Wyatt took one last look at the birdhouse, feeling that special thrill of achieving something.

Now that you are seven, you're learning that patience
and taking time to learn can help you build amazing things
—just like Wyatt and Grandpa's birdhouse.

SECRET SPY MISSION

Brandon and Eric crouched low in the bushes, eyes scanning the park ahead. Today was their biggest mission yet. Their friend Emi, the mastermind behind the "Spy Club," had left them a mysterious message that morning: "Agents, today's mission is top secret. Meet at the old oak tree by 3:00, and remember, trust is your biggest tool."

Brandon's heart raced with excitement—and a twinge of worry. He and Eric had been preparing all week, but as the mission came closer, doubts started creeping in. *What if they couldn't crack the clues? What if he let his partner down?* He glanced at Eric, who was pretending to scan the area with imaginary spy goggles, his face full of determination.

They reached the giant oak tree, where a bright red envelope labeled 'TOP SECRET' was peeking out from behind a rock. Brandon snatched it up, heart pounding, and opened it with Eric peering over his shoulder. Inside, in Emi's messy handwriting, was a message: *"Agents, the final clue is hidden somewhere in the playground. You'll need to trust each other to figure out where. Good luck!"*

Brandon's mind whirred as he thought of places to start. "Let's try the swings or the slide!" he said confidently, already picturing his plan in action.

But Eric hesitated, with a thoughtful expression on his face. "I think we're supposed to look somewhere we don't usually go. Emi told us to trust each other, right? Maybe we're supposed to go to a spot that's not as obvious."

Eric pointed toward the rock climbing wall. "How about there?"

Brandon felt his stomach tighten. The swings and slides made so much more sense! But Emi's message echoed in his mind: *Trust is your biggest tool.* He tried to keep his mind open. "Alright," he said slowly, "let's check over there."

As they walked over, Brandon felt a bit bothered. What if we're wasting our time here? *What if I've let Eric lead us off track?* They searched the base of the wall, feeling around and even peeking into the little holes in the structure, but... nothing. Brandon felt disappointed, and his annoyance was building up.

Eric glanced at him, a little embarrassed. "Maybe... maybe I got it wrong," he said, rubbing the back of his neck.

24

Brandon bit his lip, his mind racing. Part of him wanted to go back to his plan, but he forced himself to stay calm. "It's okay," he said, trying to sound more confident than he felt. "Where do you think we should try next?"

Eric's face brightened with a flash of inspiration. "The sandbox! I remember Emi hanging out there with something red the other day. It's gotta be it!"

Brandon wasn't so sure and felt the doubt rise up again. His gut told him they should just go back to the slide, but he pushed that feeling away because he wanted to give others a chance, too. "Okay... sandbox it is," he agreed, fighting the urge to sigh.

They crouched in the sandbox, sifting through the sand carefully. Brandon's fingers dug deep, hoping with every inch to feel something hidden. But after a few minutes of searching, still... nothing. *This is so frustrating!* he thought.

Eric looked disappointed, too, his shoulders slumping. "Maybe... maybe I'm just not good at this spy stuff," he mumbled.

Brandon took a deep breath from his stomach, his mind still buzzing with doubt. This was supposed to be his mission, too, wasn't it? But seeing Eric look like he was giving up made him feel something else—determination. He forced himself to shake off the doubt and think. *Trust your team, Brandon.* He looked at Eric and gave him a small smile. "We'll figure it out," he said with more hope than he felt. "Any more ideas?"

Eric stood up a bit straighter and pointed toward the picnic tables near a big tree. "What if it's over there? Emi was hiding something around the big tree the last time we all played hide and seek."

Brandon's legs were getting tired, and he was almost ready to give up. But then he saw the hopeful look in Eric's eyes, and it gave him a small spark of energy. Brandon nodded. "Alright, let's check the tree by the picnic tables."

As they walked over, his mind filled with questions. *What if we've been wrong this whole time? What if Emi thinks we're not good teammates and ends the mission?* And then, a new worry crept in: *What if I shouldn't have trusted Eric's ideas after all?*

When they reached the tree, Brandon scanned every nook and cranny, feeling the leaves crunch under his shoes as he circled it. Then, just as he was about to lose hope, he spotted a flash of red sticking out from between two roots at the base of the tree.

"Eric!" he shouted, his voice full of excitement. They dropped to their knees, and Brandon carefully pulled out a folder with 'TOP SECRET' scrawled across the front.

Just then, Emi jumped out from behind a nearby bush with a huge grin. "Agents! You did it!" she shouted, clapping her hands.

The doubts, the frustration, the moments Brandon questioned Eric—all of it faded in an instant! He and Eric had cracked the mission together, just like real spies.

Emi gave them both a high-five. "You trusted each other, and it worked!" she said, beaming.

As they walked home, Brandon couldn't help but grin, feeling closer to his friends than ever before. And he knew that their spy club would only be stronger because of this adventure.

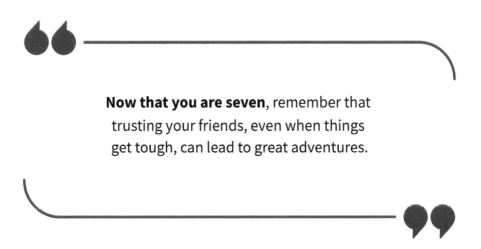

Now that you are seven, remember that trusting your friends, even when things get tough, can lead to great adventures.

HOMEWORK TIME TRAVELER

Zachary dropped his backpack on the floor and kicked off his shoes. Although it was only Monday, he was already planning his weekend. Soccer, video games, and maybe even a bike ride with his friends. That's when he saw his homework poking out of his bag. Ugh, the last thing he wanted to think about was that! Especially homework about past events in history. *Who cares about things that happened forever ago?*

"Zachary!" his mom called from the kitchen. "It's time to do your homework."

Zachary sighed, plopping down at the table with the two-page printout Mr. Wells had given them. "It's just ...so...boring," he mumbled as he looked at the first page to read the title. This first reading assignment was on ancient Egypt. *Why do I have to learn about things that already happened?*

Reluctantly, he began reading. The first line talked about a bustling marketplace under the hot Egyptian sun, where people traded goods and shared stories. As Zachary's eyes moved over the words, he felt his lids getting heavier—and then, in a blink, he was there!

Sand crunched under his feet, and the sun blazed above. He was standing in the middle of a crowded marketplace, the smell of spices tickling his nose. People were bartering, shouting out prices and goods, and carts filled with jars and fruits rolled by. "Whoa!" Zachary exclaimed, turning in amazement.

A girl near him laughed. "What's the matter? Never been to the marketplace before?" she asked, her hands full of colorful scarves.

Zachary shook his head. "Not exactly. Are those...for sale?" he asked, pointing at the scarves.

"Of course," she said with a grin. "We sell or trade what we make and what we grow. And today, we're going to see the royal procession!"

Zachary blinked, confused, as she turned to join the crowd gathering along a sandy path.

And then suddenly, he was back at his kitchen table, the pages staring up at him. He looked around, feeling the pulse of excitement in his chest. Had he really been... there?

The next day, after school, he found himself wondering what story Mr. Wells had assigned this time. As he pulled the pages out of his backpack and sat back on his bed, he saw it was about ancient Greece. "Great, more old stuff," he muttered, but a twinge of curiosity crept into his mind.

This time, as he read about grand marble statues and fancy feasts, his room seemed to melt away. Suddenly, he was surrounded by tall columns, delicious shiny grapes piled high on platters, and people in white robes. The air was filled with laughter and music, and Zachary found himself near a boy about his age, watching some men training nearby.

"What are they doing?" Zachary asked, mesmerized.

The boy raised an eyebrow. "Training, of course! The Olympics are coming up."

"The Olympics?" Zachary watched as the men raced each other and threw large stones, their faces intense and focused. "That's so cool! Do you train, too?"

The boy laughed, nodding. "Someday, I want to be the fastest in all of Greece!"

Zachary felt a warmth spread through his body. Here was a kid just like him, with dreams and goals. Before he could ask more, the world around him shifted, and he was back on his bed, his heart still pounding.

By the third day, Zachary didn't even groan when his mom reminded him of his reading homework. He grabbed the pages eagerly, and today's lesson was about the Wild West. As he read about cowboys and dusty towns, he barely noticed that his room again faded, and he found himself on an actual dusty path, a horse trotting beside him.

A cowboy tipped his hat at Zachary. "Howdy, partner," he said, handing Zachary a rope. "Think you're up for a little lasso practice?"

Zachary took the rope, feeling the rough twine under his fingers. "I…I think so?" He watched the cowboy expertly loop the lasso and tried to copy him, feeling the thrill of the open fields. Dust rose under his boots, and he lassoed over and over again. *I'm a cowboy!* But just as he got the hang of the lasso, he was snapped back to his desk, the pages still in his hands.

"Zachary!" his mom called from the living room. "It's past your bedtime!"

"Oops!" he said softly, realizing he'd been lost in the reading for far longer than he'd thought. But as he tucked the pages back into his homework folder, he felt a new kind of appreciation, a new understanding of the past. History wasn't so boring after all.

The next day at school, Zachary rushed up to Mr. Wells. "Mr. Wells! I think…I think I went back in time! I was in Egypt, and then in Greece, and then the Wild West!"

Mr. Wells chuckled as he smiled. "That's the magic of history, Zachary. The stories of the past have the power to take us on adventures without ever leaving our seats."

Zachary grinned, feeling a bit proud, as he realized that reading could be full of adventures—it wasn't just a bunch of boring words! And because Zachary wanted to go on more adventures into the past, his mom took him to the library to find some books!

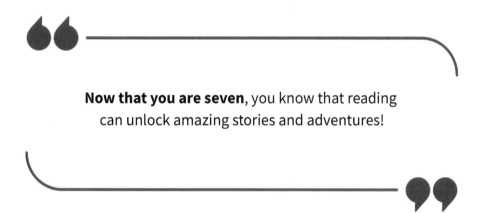

Now that you are seven, you know that reading can unlock amazing stories and adventures!

THE DISHES DUEL

Aiden eyed the mountain of dishes by the sink and sighed. His dad had just announced it was time to tackle the after-dinner cleanup, and Aiden could already feel the boredom settling in. *Why do I have to help? Washing dishes is the most boring thing ever!* He looked over at his dad, hoping for an escape.

"Alright, Aiden," his dad said, rolling up his sleeves with a grin. "How about a little Dishes Duel? I'll wash, you dry, and stack. Think you can keep up?"

Aiden frowned, crossing his arms. "A duel? With dishes?" He gave his dad a skeptical look, not quite convinced. Chores weren't supposed to be games. But his dad just raised his eyebrows and handed him a towel, ready to start.

"Come on," his dad nudged him. "Or are you too chicken for a challenge?"

Aiden narrowed his eyes playfully. He couldn't back down now, not with his dad looking so eager. "Alright," he said, grabbing the towel, "you're on!"

His dad turned on the faucet, filling the sink with warm, soapy water, and Aiden positioned himself beside the counter, actually looking forward to it. "First plate, coming your way!" his dad called, sliding a wet dish toward him.

Aiden snatched it up and started drying, determined to keep up. "Got it!" he said, setting the plate down. But before he knew it, another dish was already in his hands. Aiden dried furiously, trying to go faster. *This is kinda fun!* He thought to himself.

They kept going back and forth. His dad washed quickly, and Aiden dried and stacked as fast as he could. His hands moved in a blur as he tried to keep up with his dad's speed. But as the pile of dishes seemed to grow, Aiden felt his arms getting tired. This was harder than he'd thought!

"You sure you can keep up?" his dad teased, passing him another cup.

Aiden smiled, catching his breath. "I've got this, Dad! Just you watch!"

The game was heating up. Dishes kept coming, each one a little challenge, and they both couldn't stop laughing. Aiden felt his competitive spirit kick in even more.

Just then, his dad handed him another plate, and as Aiden grabbed it, his towel slipped a little, causing the plate to shake in his hands. His heart skipped a beat. If he dropped it, he'd be out of the duel for sure! Quickly, he steadied his grip, holding his breath as he carefully dried it and set it down. "Phew!" he muttered, glancing at his dad, who gave him a quick wink.

"You're doing an awesome job, kiddo!" his dad said, passing him another cup. "But don't slow down now!"

The dishes dwindled down to the last few, and while Aiden's arms ached, he wasn't about to quit now. Just when he thought he'd won, his dad handed him a small teaspoon, still wet.

Aiden stared at the spoon, then burst out laughing. "That's not even fair, Dad!" he said, shaking his head. Dad shrugged as if he had no idea what Aiden was talking about.

"All's fair in a Dishes Duel!" Dad replied with a smirk, passing the final plate.

Aiden wiped the spoon in a single swipe, then tackled the last plate with a fancy flick of the towel. "Done!" he shouted, raising his arms in triumph. He looked around at the sparkling clean counter and the neat stacks of dishes and felt a surprising sense of accomplishment.

"Not too bad, huh?" his dad said, throwing him up in the air suddenly. "You handled that duel pretty well!"

"Yeah, it wasn't too bad!" Aiden said, feeling the joy of victory. Chores had started out as the last thing he wanted to do, but somehow, with Dad's challenge, it was so much fun! Aiden realized that chores weren't just about getting things done—they could be a way to laugh and spend time together.

As they walked out of the kitchen, Aiden's mom passed by with a laundry basket, heading for the washing machine. Aiden looked at her and, without even thinking, said, "Hey, Mom, want to have a Laundry Duel?"

Mom raised an eyebrow, surprised. "A Laundry Duel, huh? Well, I think I'm up for the challenge!"

Aiden laughed, imagining all the ways they could make even that chore into a game! He felt ready for the next round of challenges now that he knew they didn't have to be boring.

Now that you are seven, you know that
sharing tasks with others can make
the work easier—and a lot more fun!

THE PET-SITTING ADVENTURE

"Pickles, come back!" Cody sprinted across the backyard as the little poodle darted toward the open gate. Pickles wiggled through the opening, sniffing the grass like he'd just found a hidden treasure.

Cody jumped forward, managing to scoop Pickles up just before he could escape. "Phew, that was close," he said, holding the squirmy dog close. Pickles wriggled in his arms, his tongue hanging out as if this was all a game.

Cody's dad laughed from the porch. "Looks like you've got your hands full, pet-sitter!" he teased.

Cody grinned but felt a small ball of worry in his stomach. Mr. Perez, their neighbor, had trusted him to watch Pickles for the afternoon. He'd thought pet-sitting would be easy, but Pickles seemed to have other plans. *Stay calm, I can do this,* Cody thought, giving himself a pep talk. He took a deep breath and set Pickles back down.

Inside, Mr. Perez quickly went over the instructions. "Feed him at noon, and make sure he stays in the backyard if you take him outside, and… well, he's a little high-energy, so just keep an eye on him." He laughed, scratching Pickles behind the ears. "Think you're up for it?"

"Yes, sir!" Cody replied, standing a little taller. *I'm practically a pet expert,* he told himself, though he wasn't feeling so sure anymore.

As Mr. Perez left, Cody turned to the poodle. "Okay, Pickles, let's make sure everything goes smoothly."

But the moment Mr. Perez was gone, Pickles zipped around the room, barking at the couch cushions like they were his mortal enemies. Cody laughed nervously. "Alright, time for lunch, little guy."

In the kitchen, Cody filled Pickles's bowl with dog chow, hoping it would calm the dog down. But as soon as he placed the bowl on the floor, Pickles trotted over, sniffed it once, and promptly decided he wasn't interested. Instead, he dashed toward the living room, jumping up on the couch.

Cody sighed. "Come on, Pickles, you need to eat!" He grabbed a handful of chow, holding it out as he coaxed the dog back toward the bowl. *This is harder than I imagined,* he thought, feeling his patience start to wear out.

Pickles finally took a few bites, but then he zipped away again, tearing through the house like a tiny furry tornado! Just then, Cody heard a *CRASH!* He sprang to his feet as he realized that Pickles had knocked over a vase on the coffee table!

Stay calm, Cody reminded himself. He picked up the pieces and looked over at Pickles, who was watching him with big, innocent eyes. "You're trouble, you know that?" he said, trying not to laugh.

After tidying up, Cody decided to take Pickles outside to let off some steam and to share a few dog treats with him. He double-checked that the gate was closed, then watched as Pickles ran in circles, his short legs moving as fast as they could go.

But while Cody was distracted for just a second, a strong breeze blew the side gate open. Pickles saw his chance and ran toward freedom.

"Pickles!" Cody yelled, his heart leaping into his throat. He sprinted after the dog, arms reaching out as he tried to catch him. Pickles was quick, dodging around bushes and heading straight for the sidewalk. Cody's mind raced. *If I lose him, Mr. Perez will be so upset!*

Thinking fast, Cody grabbed the treat bag from his pocket and shook it. "Pickles! Look what I've got!" he called, trying to sound calm even though his heart was racing. Pickles paused, sniffing the air, and trotted back, his eyes fixed on the treat bag.

"Gotcha!" Cody said, scooping him up and hugging him tightly. He carried Pickles back inside, closing the gate securely behind them.

Back in the living room, Cody sat on the floor, huffing and puffing. "You're a lot of work, you know that?" he said, patting Pickles on his smooth back. Pickles tilted his head, looking up at Cody with the cutest puppy dog eyes. *I've totally got this!* he said to himself happily.

He decided to give Pickles another chance with lunch. This time, the dog sniffed the bowl and started eating, his tail wagging happily. Cody smiled, feeling like maybe he was starting to get the hang of this pet-sitting thing after all.

Finally, the afternoon came to an end, and Mr. Perez returned. He looked around, noticing the vase was missing from the table. "Everything go okay?" he asked, raising an eyebrow with a curious smile.

Cody chuckled, scratching the back of his head. "There were… a few adventures," he admitted, feeling a little embarrassed.

Mr. Perez laughed, patting Cody's shoulder. "That's the Pickles experience for you. He's a handful, but *you* handled it well."

Just as Mr. Perez was about to leave, Pickles leaped up to Cody and nudged his hand, looking up at him with those big, friendly eyes. Cody felt a warm, happy feeling inside. *I actually did it,* he thought, realizing he had kept things running smoothly and made Pickles feel safe and happy.

As Mr. Perez thanked him, he said, "You did a fantastic job, Cody. Pickles seems to really like you!"

Cody smiled, giving Pickles one last scratch on his back where he seemed to like it. He had learned that taking care of someone wasn't always easy, but it sure felt good to finish what he started and feel super useful as well!

Now that you are seven, you know that being responsible means taking care of others, even when things get tricky. Finishing what you start makes you a real helper!

THE TREEHOUSE CLUB

"Tap-tap, tap-tap-tap!" Logan knocked on the treehouse door in the secret rhythm they'd come up with just last week. A few muffled laughs and whispers from inside confirmed the club was meeting as planned. He felt proud to be part of something special, something only the closest friends knew about.

"It's Logan!" he called, pushing open the door and climbing in. Jake and the others were already huddled in a circle beaming.

Jake leaned over, "I think we need to talk about David."

Logan's heart dropped a bit. David was the new kid who'd moved in a few houses down from him, and Jake's next-door neighbor. Logan had noticed him hanging around at recess or watching them play tag in the yard, waving once or twice. But Logan hadn't paid him much attention.

"What about David?" Logan asked, trying to sound casual.

Jake's face softened. "I think he's lonely. He doesn't have anyone to hang out with yet."

Logan just shrugged his shoulders. The treehouse was supposed to be special, a place where only the closest friends were allowed. Being part of something special felt exciting and cool. But when he thought about David watching from the sidelines, a little guilt crept in, making him wonder how it felt to be the one left out.

"Look, we have our club," Logan said, trying to convince himself more than anyone. "Besides, David doesn't even know about it."

But even as he spoke, he remembered David's hopeful face, watching them from a distance. Jake gave him a nudge. "I just thought it'd be nice. Maybe he could join us sometime."

Logan sighed, feeling confused. The treehouse club had always been for just a few of them, a place to keep secrets and play games only they knew. But the idea of leaving David out began to feel really tricky.

That afternoon, as they started their club games, Logan was distracted, thinking about David. He missed a key turn in their game and fell backward, knocking over the basket with all their snacks. The snacks tumbled out of the treehouse, scattering across the yard below. "No!" Logan shouted, reaching out too late to catch the tumbling pile.

Jake looked out the window. "David's out there!" he whispered. Sure enough, David was in his yard next door, and he'd seen everything. Logan's heart raced.

"Oh, no," Logan said quietly, looking back at Jake.

Logan felt a surge of panic. Their club was no longer a secret, and they couldn't ignore David now.

"Should we invite him up?" Jake asked, hopeful but hesitant.

Logan paused. He really wanted the club to stay just for them. Thoughts swirled in his head. *What if David didn't fit in? What if he wasn't fun? What if he bossed everyone around?* But then he remembered how lonely David had looked before, and his heart softened. After a deep breath, he waved to David, calling out, "Hey, want to come up?"

A grin instantly spread across David's face as he happily climbed the tree, joining them for the first time. Logan felt uncomfortable, unsure how things would go and if it was the right choice.

As David sat down, he looked around the treehouse with awe. "This is so cool!" he said, his face lighting up. "Thanks so much for asking me up!"

David quickly fit right in. He showed them a funny handshake he'd learned from his old school, and they all laughed trying it out. Then, David told them about his favorite game—a treasure hunt where they'd hide clues and have to find the hidden "treasure." "That sounds awesome!" said Jake, while Logan felt his own nervousness fading away.

They spent the rest of the afternoon planning the treasure hunt. David hid the first clue, and they all scrambled around, searching every corner of the yard and treehouse, laughing each time someone found a clue. When Logan uncovered the "treasure" at the end—a shiny, painted rock David had brought as a prize—their cheers echoed through the yard.

As the sun began to set, the group sat in the treehouse, happily munching on what was left of the snacks. Logan looked around at his friends, feeling something new—a feeling of happiness that hadn't been there before.

When Logan walked home that night, he glanced back at the treehouse, heart full to the top. He realized that sometimes, adding a new friend didn't mean losing something special. It just made it even better. Plus, it felt so good to make someone else happy.

50

Now that you are seven, remember that sharing and
including others makes friendships stronger,
and we know we should treat others how we'd
like to be treated. Sometimes, adding new friends
to our circle brings in new ideas and fun moments
we'd never have experienced without them.

THE GARDEN GROWERS

"Mom, can we plant a garden? I want to grow the biggest, juiciest carrots ever!" Carter announced one day, gripping his new packet of seeds like it was a precious gift.

His mom chuckled and went to the little garden shed. After rustling about, she handed him a small shovel. "A garden, huh? That sounds fun! But remember, growing a garden takes patience and a lot of care. Once you get started, you have to keep looking after it."

"I will!" Carter replied. He could already picture rows of tall tomatoes, leafy lettuce, and bright orange carrots filling their backyard. But his mom suggested they start with just one vegetable to learn how to take care of it first. "Let's try carrots this time," she said, smiling. "We can add more once you've got the hang of it."

Nodding excitedly, Carter agreed. He loved carrots, and he knew he would especially love the ones he'd grown himself! Together, they found the sunniest spot in the yard, and Carter got to work, digging tiny holes for each carrot seed and then carefully placing them in the ground like precious treasures.

"Do you think they'll grow by tomorrow?" Carter asked, sprinkling soil over the last few seeds.

His mom giggled. "Not quite that fast, buddy. But if we water them every day, check the soil, and let the sun do its job, it won't be long before you'll see them sprout."

Every morning, Carter rushed to his garden; he couldn't wait to spot the first signs of life. But after a whole week of careful watering and lots and lots of watching, the soil looked just as bare as the day he planted the seeds! He kneeled down beside the tiny plot, frowning as he poked a small hole in the soil with his finger. "Come on, little carrots," he whispered, "where are you?"

He sighed, a bit disappointed. "Why aren't they growing, Mom?"

She kneeled down beside him. "Plants are a little bit like you, Carter. They take time to grow. But they are well worth it when they do! Just keep caring for them, and they'll surprise you."

Carter nodded, though he wasn't convinced. Still, he watered his garden every day, even on the chilly mornings, and carefully made sure there were no weeds sneaking in.

One bright morning, as he was sprinkling water over the soil, Carter noticed something small and green poking out.

"A sprout!" he shouted. His heart leaped with excitement, and he ran to get his mom. "Look! It's working! My garden is growing!"

His mom smiled proudly. "See? All that patience is paying off."

Every day, the sprout grew a little bigger, and soon, more tiny green stems started to pop up around it. Carter's excitement and happiness grew just as every new leaf grew, each like a little cheer for his hard work.

Then, one afternoon, a big rainstorm rolled in. Lightning flashed, thunder rumbled, and then BOOM BOOM! Heavy raindrops hammered the ground. Carter watched from the window, worried about his little sprouts. *Will they be okay?*

The next morning, he ran outside; his heart dropped as he spotted his garden. The rain had washed some of the soil away, leaving his plants drooping, their stems bent and muddy.

"Oh no, Mom! My plants… they look like they're hurt."

His mom joined him, crouching down beside the messy soil. "They look a bit tired and droopy, don't they? But they're pretty strong, and they have those long roots growing down under the soil, holding them tight. Let's help them get cozy again."

Carefully, Carter patted the soil back around each sprout, softly giving words of encouragement to them. "Come on, little guys. Don't give up. You can keep growing!"

The next few days, he gave his plants extra care, watering them gently and even shielding them with an umbrella when another drizzle began. And sure enough, the plants perked up, stretching their leaves toward the sun once more.

A few weeks later, Carter's garden was a burst of green, and his favorite part had arrived—the harvest.

"I can't believe they are ready!" said Carter.

His mom showed him how to gently tug on the carrot tops, and his eyes widened as the first long, orange carrot popped out of the ground.

"WHOA, look! It's huge!" He held up the carrot triumphantly, feeling like he'd just uncovered buried gold.

They spent the afternoon gathering the carrots, each one a reward for all the waiting and hard work. As they laid them out, Carter couldn't help but smile proudly at what they'd grown together.

"This was so worth it," he said, holding the biggest carrot of all. "I didn't know growing things could feel this good."

"You took such good care of your garden, Carter. And look how it turned out! I'm super proud of you. But I think you've forgotten something…"

"Oh! Yes! CRUNCH!" Carter took a big bite of his carrot as he looked out over his garden, feeling a special kind of happiness. He knew that it wasn't just the carrots that had grown—he had, too.

Now that you are seven, you're learning that
patience and care can help things grow—
just like your own garden. The best rewards come
when you stick with something and watch it bloom!
Don't forget to be patient with your own growth, too!

TALLEST TOWER CHALLENGE

There was a special energy in the classroom today. The tables were pushed aside, and buckets of colorful blocks were stacked in the center, ready for Mr. Griffin's big announcement. Each team of two had its own space and pile of blocks, and the kids were already eyeing their stacks, chatting about their plans.

This is going to be so much fun! Elliot thought.

Mr. Griffin stood at the front, holding a clipboard and grinning. "All right, everyone! Today's challenge is to build the tallest tower you can. You'll have exactly fifteen minutes!"

The students cheered, and no one was louder than Elliot. He looked over at Bryce, his best friend and teammate, who was already planning their strategy. He could almost feel the trophy in his hands.

Mr. Griffin glanced at his watch, raising his voice over the chatter. "Remember, builders, your tower has to stand on its own for one full minute. Ready, set—go!"

Elliot grabbed the first block, already visualizing a towering skyscraper. He quickly stacked a few blocks, his mind spinning with ideas. But as he reached for another block, Bryce gave him a nudge.

"Careful, Elliot," said Bryce, "We need it to stay steady."

Elliot barely heard him, his mind already racing ahead. *If I build fast enough, no one else will get close,* he thought, stacking block after block on top of each other. The whole room buzzed with activity as the other kids worked on their own towers, but Elliot and Bryce were already reaching the halfway mark. Elliot could feel the thrill building up inside him. *We are so going to win this!*

But just as he was about to place another block, he noticed the tower wobbling. "Uh-oh!" Bryce warned, a worried look on his face.

Before Elliot could react—*CRASH!*—the entire tower crumbled, blocks scattering in every direction. His stomach dropped, and his face turned bright red. He could feel the eyes of his classmates on him, some whispering, some giggling. He'd never felt so embarrassed!

"Elliot, are you okay?" Bryce asked, giving him a gentle nudge.

Mr. Griffin walked over, smiling. "Building something strong takes patience, Elliot. Why don't you two try again?"

Elliot shrugged, but he could feel a tightness in his chest. He wanted to win so badly, but now his tower was just a pile of blocks on the floor. *This was supposed to be easy,* he thought, tightening his fists. His face turned bright red as he heard a few gasps and giggles around the room.

Bryce knelt to help pick up the blocks. "We can try again," he said softly, patting Elliot on the back.

Elliot sighed, feeling both embarrassed and frustrated. He wanted to shout, *But we were supposed to win!* But he bit his tongue, looking at Bryce, who was patiently rebuilding the base.

"Eight minutes left!" Mr. Griffin called.

The room was now filled with shouts of "Whoa!" and "Look at ours!" from other teams. Elliot looked around, his nerves sparking. Some of the other groups had already reached the table height, maybe even taller.

"Bryce, we need to hurry," Elliot said, his voice tight. "Let's just add these fast—"

But Bryce shook his head. "Remember last time? If we go too fast, it'll just fall again."

Elliot took a deep breath, his stomach churning. He wanted to have the tallest tower, to see theirs soar above everyone else's. But he also didn't want to see it crash again.

Reluctantly, he nodded, pressing his lips together and focusing on each block, one by one. He could feel his hands shaking, the tension building inside him with every new piece.

"Almost there!" Bryce said excitedly as their tower neared the top of the table.

But suddenly, a loud crash sounded from the team next to them. Elliot's heart raced as he saw their tower come tumbling down, blocks flying everywhere. He exchanged a wide-eyed glance with Bryce.

"See? That's what happens when you rush," Bryce whispered, giving Elliot an encouraging nod.

Elliot managed a small smile. *Just a few more blocks,* he thought, feeling the thrill of being so close. His fingers tingled as he carefully placed another block.

"Ten seconds!" Mr. Griffin counted down, and Elliot placed the last block.

The room went silent as Mr. Griffin came over, counting down the seconds. "Ten… nine… eight…"

Elliot held his breath, his eyes fixed on the tower. The blocks wobbled, but each one held its place.

"Three… two… one… Time!"

The tower stood firm, and Elliot's heart puffed with pride. "We did it, Bryce!" he cheered, high-fiving his friend.

The whole class clapped as Mr. Griffin walked over. "Well done, Elliot and Bryce! The tallest tower of the day!"

As the class clapped, Elliot felt grateful he hadn't given up or let his impatience take over. With a smile, he looked over at Bryce, who gave him a big thumbs-up. Encouraging friends sure help too!

Now that you are seven, you know that sometimes, taking your time and working together is the best way to build something amazing!

MISSING BASEBALL GLOVE

After placing his sports bag on the bleachers, Flynn was ready to grab his baseball glove and head to the field. But when he opened the bag, "Oh, no!" His glove wasn't there. He rummaged through everything—his bat, cleats, cap—but still no glove.

"No way..." he muttered, digging through the bag again. His lucky glove was missing! This was his favorite glove, the one Grandpa gave him with his initials stitched on the thumb.

Flynn glanced over at his friend Dylan, who was warming up nearby. "Dylan, have you seen my glove? I'm sure I packed it..."

Dylan shook his head, a little puzzled. "You had it yesterday at practice. Maybe you left it at home?"

Flynn thought back to the day before. He could picture himself tossing the ball with Dylan, laughing as they practiced curveballs. But then...where had he put it afterward? He felt a worried feeling in his stomach as he realized he might've left it somewhere by mistake. Coach Dan noticed Flynn lingering by the bleachers.

"Everything okay, Flynn?" his coach asked.

"My glove is missing..." Flynn admitted. He worried that his coach might think he'd been careless.

Coach nodded thoughtfully. "Maybe retrace your steps; see if it turns up. We'll start practicing in a few minutes."

Flynn tried to stay calm. *Alright, retrace my steps,* he said to himself, holding his bag tightly. *Now, where did I have it last?*

Flynn took a deep breath, scanning the field. He ran over to the fence where he'd sat yesterday, crouching down to search the grass. Nothing. The worried feeling in his stomach turned into a twisting knot.

Dylan jogged over to help. "Still no sign of it? Let's check the dugout!" They looked in the dugout, checked around the equipment, and even peeked behind the water cooler. Still nothing.

This glove is too special to lose, Flynn thought sadly, swallowing the lump in his throat. Grandpa had given it to him after his first big game, telling him it was for "good luck and lots of practice." Flynn could still hear Grandpa's voice in his head, reminding him to always keep an eye on his things.

Then Dylan snapped his fingers. "What about the clubhouse? Sometimes people turn in stuff they find."

Flynn's face lit up. "Good idea! Let's go check!" The two raced to the clubhouse.

"Please be there," he said as he pushed open the door.

Flynn's hands were clammy as he approached the front desk. "Excuse me," he said in a rush, "Did anyone hand in a baseball glove?"

The lady at the counter raised an eyebrow, then reached under the desk with a smile. "Would this be it?"

Flynn's eyes widened as he saw his initials on the thumb. "Yes! That's it!" he said, barely containing his excitement. He grinned from ear to ear as he held it. He felt such a relief as he squeezed the glove tight, vowing to never lose it again.

Back on the field, Flynn joined practice with a spring in his step. He felt a little silly for being careless but knew this was a reminder to take better care of things that mattered.

At Saturday's game, it was the last inning, with two outs, and Flynn's team was only just holding onto their lead. The other team's batter stepped up, and Flynn's heart raced as he focused intently, his precious glove ready.

The batter swung, and the ball soared high into the sky, heading right toward Flynn. He tracked it, feeling the weight of his glove. Steadying himself, he reached out and, with a solid *THWACK*, caught the ball right in the center of his glove!

The crowd erupted in cheers, and Flynn looked to the bleachers. There was Grandpa, giving him a proud smile and a big thumbs-up. Flynn grinned back, thinking that this moment wouldn't have felt half as special if he'd lost his glove! That's when he knew just how grateful he was to have his glove right where it belonged.

Now that you are seven, remember that taking care of special things shows you're responsible and grateful for them, and that's part of growing up!

THE WOBBLY WHEEL

"Come on, Mateo!" Felix shouted, zooming by on his bike. "You're finally riding with us to school!"

Mateo grinned back, holding his handlebars tight as he started pedaling down the street. His new bike felt awesome—shiny red with smooth brakes and a cool bell he couldn't wait to ring. But as he picked up speed, he noticed his bike wobbling slightly. His grip tightened, and he reminded himself, *Stay steady. Don't mess up.*

The other kids were already ahead, riding in smooth lines like they'd been doing it forever. Mateo leaned forward, determined to catch up. He was thrilled to finally be part of the group; no longer the kid left walking as they zoomed off each morning. But as he pedaled hard to keep up, his front wheel veered a little to the side, and he nearly clipped a hedge.

"OH! That was close!" he muttered, catching his balance just in time. Mateo's heart did a somersault, and he felt his face flush when he heard a couple of kids giggle. Trying to brush it off, he pedaled even harder, but his bike kept wobbling.

Felix looked back, noticing Mateo was struggling. "You're doing great, Mateo! Just keep steady!" he called out with a thumbs-up.

Mateo tried to smile, but he could feel a heavy pit of worry in his stomach. *Why can't I keep my bike straight?* he wondered, glancing down at his handlebars. They were firm and steady, but his hands were starting to ache from holding on so tight. Every time he looked up, he felt the wobble get worse. *Maybe I'm just not cut out for riding with the others…*

When they finally reached the school bike racks, Mateo's relief was cut short as his front wheel hit a small bump on the sidewalk. He jolted forward, almost toppling over before catching himself. He put his head down quickly as Felix and the others ran over to help. He couldn't shake the embarrassment that filled him as they locked up their bikes. "It's fine," he mumbled, forcing a smile. "I just need more practice."

The ride home wasn't much better. Mateo trailed behind the group, his excitement replaced by frustration. He wanted so badly to fit in, to ride confidently beside his friends, but all he felt was shaky and out of place!

That afternoon, Mateo slumped down in the kitchen, his bike helmet dangling in his hand. His dad noticed and pulled up a chair beside him. "Rough day with the new wheels?"

Mateo sighed, nodding. "Everyone else just rides so smoothly. I keep wobbling like I'm gonna tip over!" His dad nodded. "I thought it'd be easy, but I'm just messing it up."

His dad gave him a thoughtful smile. "You know, I had some wobbly starts when I first learned, too," he said. "How about we head to the quiet path down by the park and do some practice rides?"

Mateo perked up a bit. Practicing without the pressure of keeping up sounded… great. He nodded, grabbing his helmet. "Okay. Let's go."

At the park, Mateo and his dad rode side by side on the empty path. Each time he pedaled, Mateo's dad cheered him on, helping him relax his grip and focus on the steady rhythm of his pedaling. The quietness of the path and not having to keep up made it easier to concentrate, and as he rode, Mateo started to feel more confident.

"See?" his dad said as Mateo managed a smooth turn without wobbling. "It's all about finding your balance."

They practiced for nearly an hour, and Mateo laughed each time he got a little better, his nervousness slowly melting away. He even managed to speed up a bit, realizing he could control the bike more easily as he got steadier.

"Thanks, Dad, that really helped," he said when they arrived back home.

The next day, Mateo climbed onto his bike, but the nerves were back, churning in his stomach like butterflies. He took a deep breath, gripping the handlebars tighter than ever. *You can do this now,* he told himself. *You've been practicing.*

But as they started riding, Mateo's bike wobbled again. He swerved a little too close to Jenna, causing her to gasp and veer off to the side. "Hey, be careful!" she called with a nervous laugh.

Mateo couldn't believe he messed up again. His fingers started to feel sweaty and shake. It felt just like yesterday: the wobbles, the imbalance, the fear of not fitting in.

Just then, he remembered what his dad had told him about focusing ahead and keeping his pace steady, not too fast. *Pretend it's just like with Dad,* he told himself, taking a deep breath.

Mateo steadied his grip and shifted his weight, feeling more grounded. He looked straight ahead, and his pedaling became smoother.

This time, as they reached the end of the block, Mateo was right alongside his friends, steady and confident. He even managed a grin as they cheered him on, feeling his confidence finally settle.

"You're riding like a pro now!" Felix said, giving him a playful punch on the arm. Mateo grinned back, his worries from yesterday completely gone. Riding with his friends, he felt confident and happy, no longer struggling to keep up.

As they locked up their bikes, Mateo spotted his dad across the street, watching with a proud smile. Mateo waved, feeling that special, happy feeling deep inside.

Now that you are seven, you know that with patience, you can master any new challenge safely and happily!

NEW TEACHER SURPRISE

The classroom hummed with hushed chatter and excitement. Luke leaned over to his friend, Grant, and whispered, "Have you seen the new substitute teacher yet? I heard she's really strict."

Grant shrugged, glancing nervously at the door. "I dunno, maybe Ms. Green just got sick?"

Just then, the door opened, and in walked Mrs. Brooks. She was tall, with her hair pulled back tightly, and she carried a big stack of papers under her arm. Her face was serious, and she looked straight ahead, almost like she didn't see any of them. Luke felt his stomach do a nervous flip. *She looks...scary,* he thought.

"Good morning, class," Mrs. Brooks said in a clear, calm voice. "Please take out your math books, and we'll get started."

Luke glanced around, his friends giving each other uncertain looks. Ms. Green usually started the day with a story, a joke, or even a silly dance. But Mrs. Brooks got right down to work, her voice firm as she led them through the lesson. It felt…different.

As she moved on to science, Luke noticed she kept her eyes on the paper in her hand, barely glancing up. *Maybe she doesn't want to be here either,* he thought, suddenly feeling sorry for her. But he wasn't sure what he could do about it.

Later at recess, Luke was playing tag when he paused to catch his breath. Just then, he heard Mrs. Brooks chatting softly with another teacher nearby. She held some papers, letting out a small sigh. "It's always tough starting in a new place. I don't know anyone here yet," she said, her voice gentle. "I just hope the kids warm up to me."

Luke's eyes widened. *She's nervous too!* he realized, surprised. All her seriousness was because she felt out of place, just like he did sometimes when he was new to things. He had an idea, but he needed his friends' help.

"Let's make her feel welcome!" Luke said, gathering his friends around after recess. "She's probably just unsure, like when we're new at something. What if we made her a 'Welcome' card?"

His friend, Tara, nodded. "And we could bring snacks! Everyone feels better with a snack!"

Soon the plan was in place. Luke and his friends worked together, making a big, colorful card that said, "Welcome, Mrs. Brooks!" They drew little hearts and stars around the words, each of them adding their own touch. Tara brought in some cookies, Grant brought a tiny flower he found on the playground, and Luke borrowed his mom's colored markers to make sure the card looked its best.

The next morning, Mrs. Brooks walked into the classroom and stopped short, her eyes widening when she saw the card and snacks waiting on her desk. Luke and his friends all stood together, a little shy but smiling.

"What's all this?" she asked, her voice soft and a bit shaky.

Luke stepped forward, his heart racing. "We wanted to welcome you, Mrs. Brooks. We know it's not easy to be new."

For a moment, Mrs. Brooks didn't say anything. She looked at the card, the cookies, and then back at the kids. Slowly, a smile spread across her face—a big, warm smile that made her look completely different.

"Thank you!" she said, her voice filled with surprise and gratitude. "This...this means a lot to me. I was a bit nervous about being here, but you've made me feel right at home." She took a cookie and bit into it, and everyone laughed as she gave them a playful thumbs-up.

From that day on, Mrs. Brooks seemed a lot more relaxed. She started their lessons with little stories about herself, sharing funny moments from her own school days, and even sang a silly song to help them remember their spelling words. Luke felt happy, knowing their kindness had helped her open up. Each day, it felt more like she was truly part of their class, and she even joined them during recess sometimes to cheer them on in their games.

When her time as a substitute ended, Mrs. Brooks gathered the class around for a little goodbye. "It's been so special being here with all of you. I'll never forget this class," she said, smiling down at them. Luke's shoulders dropped, realizing she was leaving. He looked around and saw the same sadness on his friends' faces. Tara sniffled, and Grant looked down, trying to hide his disappointment.

One month later, Luke was in class when the door opened, and in walked Mrs. Brooks! She was carrying her own bag and a stack of notebooks, just like the first day.

"Good morning, class!" she greeted, her smile as bright as ever.

Everyone stared, their mouths open in surprise.

Luke blinked. "Mrs. Brooks? Are you...staying?"

She laughed and nodded. "Yes, I'm your new full-time teacher! I couldn't stay away from my favorite class."

"Yay!" cheered the class. Soon everyone rushed to give her high-fives, hugs, and excited welcomes. *She wasn't just a teacher now; she was really part of their class. And I helped make that happen!*

Now that you are seven, remember that being kind can make anyone feel at home —even grownups. And when they feel welcome, their true kindness shines right back.

THE SECRET SUPERHERO

Super Caleb is here to save the day! he said to himself, bouncing on his toes in front of the mirror. His invisible cape, which only he could feel, swished grandly behind him. It was smooth, almost silky, hanging from his shoulders like a real superhero's. Today, he would be brave, helpful, and mysterious!

With a final tug at his 'cape,' Caleb flew outside, looking all around for his first big mission. The backyard? All clear. Front yard? Quiet. But just as he was about to move on, he heard a faint cry. He felt a burst of excitement as he spotted his younger neighbor, Oliver, tugging at his tangled tricycle chain in his driveway.

"Super Caleb, reporting for duty!" he said, rushing over, his cape 'flapping' behind him. "Need a hand, Oliver?"

Oliver nodded, looking up with sad eyes. "I can't fix it! The chain is stuck."

Caleb crouched down, pulling on his cape as if activating his super strength. "Not to worry. I've got this!" Carefully, he pulled and twisted the chain, his 'super hands' working exactly like a real hero. After a few tricky turns, the chain snapped back into place. "There you go, buddy," said Oliver happily.

"Thanks, Caleb! You like… saved the day, like a real hero!" said Oliver.

Caleb puffed his chest with pride. That was exactly the kind of response he was hoping for. He could feel his cape tighten around his shoulders, almost as though it was giving him a pat on the back. *This is what heroes do,* he thought. With a final salute to Oliver, he turned, wondering where his next mission would take him.

At school, the lunchtime buzz filled the cafeteria, and Caleb slid into his seat beside his best friend, Jin. As he opened his lunch, Caleb noticed Jin's eyes fixed on the table, his hands still. "What's wrong?" he asked, trying to keep his voice low, like a real superhero might.

Jin sighed. "I forgot my lunch."

Caleb could feel his cape warm up as if encouraging him to act. *A hero always helps a friend in need,* he thought. Reaching into his own bag, he pulled out his sandwich and split it in two, handing one half to Jin. "Here, we'll share. Problem solved!"

Jin smiled gratefully, and they clinked sandwich halves like superheroes celebrating a victory. "Thanks, Caleb. You're the best."

The pride he felt made his cape seem even bigger. But he wasn't done yet; real heroes always have a new mission.

Later, during recess, he saw Julian, a quiet boy from his class, standing alone near the swing set. Before he could even take a step toward him, a group of older kids approached, laughing and pointing at Julian's untied shoelaces, and knocked over his water bottle. Caleb's stomach felt funny when he saw the worried look on Julian's face. He knew what he had to do, but the thought of standing up to the older kids made him feel small.

No, he reminded himself, *I've got my invisible cape, and real heroes don't back down.*

He tugged again at his cape, took a deep breath, and walked over, heart thumping wildly. "Hey! Why don't you guys leave him alone?" he said, trying to sound strong. The older kids turned to him, surprised, and for a moment, Caleb thought they might laugh. But something in his voice seemed to stop them.

"Fine, whatever," one of them mumbled, rolling his eyes as they walked off.

Julian looked over, blinking in surprise. "Thanks, Caleb," he whispered, standing his water bottle back up.

"No problem," Caleb replied, flashing him a superhero smile. His cape seemed to wrap around him even tighter, giving him a warm, strong feeling. This was his favorite mission yet, and he knew it was exactly what a real hero would have done.

As the final bell rang, Caleb headed home, feeling like he'd just had the best day ever. But his adventure wasn't quite over yet. As he approached his front door, he saw his little sister, Lucy, struggling with a shoebox of art supplies, wobbling as she tried to bring it up the steps. *One more mission,* he thought, pulling at his cape.

"Need a hand, Lucy?" he asked, grabbing the box and steadying her. Together, they brought it inside, and she looked up at him and said, "You're a real-life hero, Caleb!"

That night, as he hung his invisible cape on the bedpost, Caleb thought about everything he'd done that day. He might not have flown or had super strength, but he'd learned something important—you didn't need superpowers to be a hero; you just need kindness and courage, even when it was hard.

Now that you are seven, remember that true heroes are kind and brave, even when no one's watching.

CONCLUSION

Wow, what an incredible journey you've been on, you super seven-year-old!

Through these stories, you've been on magical adventures, made new friends, tackled tricky challenges, and found out just how much you're capable of. Whether it was building something awesome, being a great teammate, or showing kindness when it mattered most, you've seen how little actions can make a big difference.

And here's the best part—there are even more adventures waiting for you! Every day as a 7-year-old is another chance to learn, grow, and have fun. You're already doing so many amazing things, and we're so proud of the person you're becoming.

When you turn eight, get ready for a brand-new book packed with even more exciting stories and lessons just for you. But until then, keep being the incredible 7-year-old you are, filled with curiosity, kindness, and courage.

Stay amazing and keep shining—we can't wait to see what you'll do next!

Bye, Bye!

The End

Made in United States
Troutdale, OR
02/04/2025

28687500R00056